Abby's Adventures
Dance Recital
...and the Case of Ballerina-itis!

written by
Suzanne Ridolfi

illustrated by
Dawn Griffin

Eifrig Publishing LLC
Berlin   Lemont

Abby and her mother strolled along Main Street admiring the store windows. There was Gilligan's, a charming bookstore, Frosty's Ice Cream Shop, and then she saw it . . .

The most wonderful
window ever!

It looked like
a sea of

pink
cotton
candy.

"Can we go see?" cried Abby.
Mother nodded yes
with a smile.

In the window were a pair of pink tights, pink ballet slippers, and a large framed picture of a ballerina holding a bouquet of pink flowers . . .

. . . and in the middle was the most *amazing* pink tutu she had ever seen.

Mother read the sign,
"Miss Nadia's Dance Studio
Now enrolling for fall classes."

"Oh, can we go inside?!" Abby squealed with delight.

The teacher greeted them at the door.
"Hello. I am Miss Nadia. Would you like a tour?"

Abby watched as Miss Nadia walked across the studio like she was floating on air, **straight** and *tall* and **perfect**.

"Are you interested in lessons?" asked Miss Nadia.

"OH, yes!!" said Abby. "I will be the best ballerina ever."

"Ballet is a lot of hard work. Go home and practice your posture and balance, and I will see you on Saturday," smiled Miss Nadia.

Abby was so excited
she could hardly sleep
Friday night.

Saturday morning,
she put on her tights
and new ballet shoes and

twirled

around her room,
eager to start.

"Class, we have a new student. Her name is Abby. Let's welcome her."

The other girls greeted her with a smile and a hello.

"Line up at the bar in *first position*."

All the other girls already knew exactly what she meant, but Miss Nadia helped Abby learn all five positions.

"Next we will practice our turns. Pick a spot on the wall and focus on it each time you turn around," instructed Miss Nadia.

The other girls made it look so *easy*.

"Abby, it's your turn," said Miss Nadia.

Abby felt *butterflies* in her tummy. She spun and spun and spun . . . right onto the floor. Her head was *dizzy* and her face was red and felt hot.

Abby was *exhausted.*
There was so much to remember.

The next week wasn't much better. She stepped on the tall girl Anna's foot, spun into the wall, and knocked over the whole row during an Arabesque.
Her head was still dizzy, her face felt hot and red again, and her tummy was still full of butterflies.

The next Saturday, Abby decided she was not good enough to be a ballerina.
It was **too hard,** and she wanted to **quit**.

"Abby," called mother.
"Are you ready for class, dear?"

Oh no, what can I do? Abby thought.

Then she saw her doll's
red lipstick ...

Mother opened the door and said, "Oh my, you look *awful.*"

"I feel awful. I think I am contagious, so I don't think I can go to ballet anymore," Abby groaned.

"I have heard of this . . . you are suffering from *ballerina-itis,*" sighed mother.

"I AM?!" exclaimed Abby.

"It is a dreadful thing ballet dancers get."

"They DO?!" winced Abby.

"Miss Nadia will know how to fix it, I'm certain," assured mother.

Mother told Miss Nadia how Abby didn't feel well and how she thought maybe she should quit ballet.

Miss Nadia took one look at Abby.

"HMMM," she said.
"Let me see if you have any other symptoms - do you sometimes feel dizzy in class, or have butterflies in your tummy, or has your face ever felt hot and when you looked in the mirror it was red?"

"Yes, YES, YES!!!
Oh my goodness, I really do have ballerina-itis," cried Abby.
"Can you fix me???"

"I most certainly can. Just stand right in front of the mirror. Close your eyes and spin one time, do a plié, and repeat after me:
'I AM A BALLERINA.'
Then open your eyes and tell me what you see," said Miss Nadia.

"I AM A BALLERINA," Abby said with a wide grin. Then her grin began to fade. "I want to be the *best* ballerina, but I'm not even a *good* ballerina," she said sadly.

"'Best' is a funny word, Abby. You don't need to be the best ballerina in the whole world . . . you just need to be the best ballerina that *you* can be, and to do that you need to

practice,
practice,
practice!!!"

Practice
she did!!

On Monday,
she **leaped**
to the bus stop.

On Tuesday,
she did an
Arabesque
in the lunch line.

And on Thursday, she spun
through the grocery store.

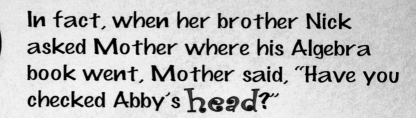

In fact, when her brother Nick asked Mother where his Algebra book went, Mother said, "Have you checked Abby's head?"

"Hey, Squirt, what are you doing?" asked Nick.

"I am practicing to be the best ballerina I can be," Abby said proudly.

The night before her big recital, Daddy peeked in Abby's bedroom door to tuck her in.

"What do we have here?" he said.

"It's Miss Abigail's Dance Studio . . . some of the students are a little **scared**," Abby answered.

"It's okay to be scared. I bet even dance teachers get nervous sometimes, but **the show must go on!**" smiled Daddy.

"Did you tell your students not to worry, just to do their **best** and have **fun?**"

"Yes, let me tell them one more time and then we will be ready."

Abby put on her beautiful tutu and studied the mirror. No signs of *ballerina-itis* - all of her practice had cured her, just like Miss Nadia had promised.

"I am ready!"
she told her students.

When the bright lights came on, Abby looked nervously into the audience. Then she remembered what Miss Nadia had said . . . *practice, practice, practice.*

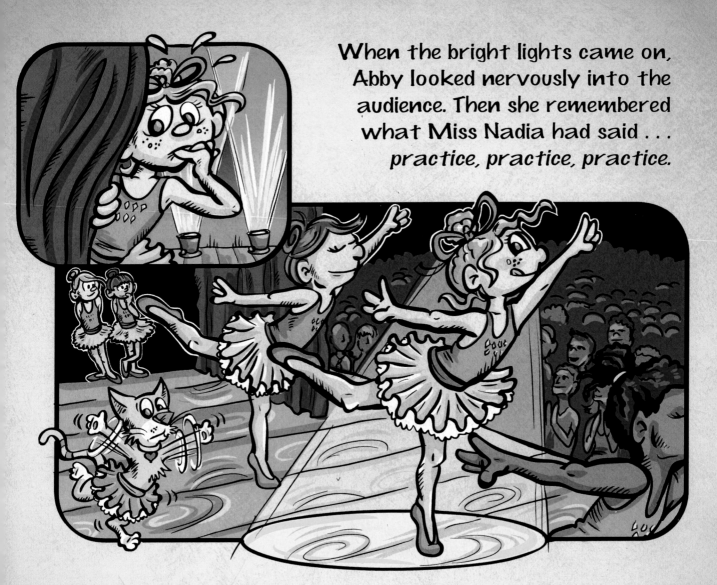

Abby remembered how **hard** she had worked. *I will try my best,* she thought. She wobbled a bit at first, then counted each step, managed to spin without falling, and did an **almost** perfect Arabesque. When the performance ended, the audience cheered!

Miss Nadia smiled and said,
"You are a *lovely ballerina*, Miss Abby.
You worked so hard,
and I am proud of you.
Now, I believe
you have some
fans waiting."

Mother, Daddy, and Nick greeted Abby with a
big beautiful bouquet of flowers that said:
"TO OUR BEST BALLERINA."

Practice makes you better, but you don't have to be THE best. It's okay to just be YOUR best!

♡♡ABBY

The End

Published by Eifrig Publishing,
PO Box 66, Lemont, PA 16851, USA
Knobelsdorffstr. 44, 14059 Berlin, Germany.

For information regarding permission, write to:
Rights and Permissions Department,
Eifrig Publishing,
PO Box 66, Lemont, PA 16851, USA.
permissions@eifrigpublishing.com, +1-888-340-6543

Library of Congress Control Data: 2012940403
  Ridolfi, Suzanne
Abby's Adventures: Dance Recital ... and the Case of Ballerina-itis!
/ by Suzanne Ridolfi, illustrated by Dawn Griffin

p. cm.

Paperback: ISBN 978-1-936172-03-0
Hardcover: ISBN 978-1-936172-04-7
Ebook: ISBN 978-1-936172-56-6

[1. Dance – Juvenille Fiction. 2. Self-image – Juvenille Fiction.]
I. Griffin, Dawn, ill. II. Title: Dance Recital ...
and the Case of Ballerina-itis!

16 15 14 13 2012
5 4 3 2 1

Printed on acid-free paper. ∞

To my husband, Joe,
my love and best friend,
who has made this
possible through his
encouragement and
constant support

S. R.

Our goal is to help each child to realize that no matter how difficult growing up may seem,

It's okay to be me!

More of Abby's Adventures:

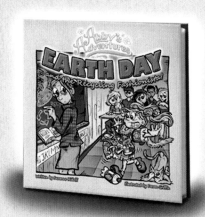

**Earth Day ...
and the Recycling Fashionista**
ISBN: 978-1-936172-15-3 (PB)
ISBN: 978-1-936172-37-5 (HC)

**Christmas Carol ...
and Little Miss Scrooge**
ISBN: 978-1-936172-42-9 (PB)
ISBN: 978-1-936172-43-6 (HC)

**Picture Day ...
and the Missing Tooth**
ISBN: 978-1-936172-08-5 (PB)
ISBN: 978-1-936172-09-2 (HC)